Boing-Boing the Bionic Cat and the Jewel Thief

Other Boing-Boing Books

Boing-Boing the Bionic Cat

Larry L. Hench, Ruth Denise Lear—Illustrator

© 2000, ISBN 1-57498-109-9

Boing-Boing
the Bionic Cat
and the Jewel Thief

by Larry L. Hench

Illustrations by Ruth Denise Lear

Published by
The American Ceramic Society
735 Ceramic Place
Westerville, Ohio 43081 USA

The American Ceramic Society
735 Ceramic Place
Westerville, Ohio 43081
www.ceramics.org

Printed in Hong Kong
First edition
09 08 07 06 05 04 03 02 01   10 9 8 7 6 5 4 3 2 1

The text of this book is set in Koch Plain. The illustrations are watercolor and ink.
This book was printed on acid-free paper and was Smyth-sewn with cotton thread.

Senior Director, Publications
Mark Mecklenborg
Acquisitions
Mary J. Cassells
Developmental Editor
Sarah Godby

Marketing Assistant
Jennifer Brewer
Production Manager
John Wilson

Library of Congress Cataloging-in-Publication Data

Hench, L. L.
    Boing-Boing the bionic cat and the jewel thief / by Larry L. Hench ; illustrations by Ruth Denise Lear.-- 1st ed.
        p. cm.
    Summary: After Professor George improves Boing-Boing the bionic cat by giving him a ceramic sensor tail that allows him to roar, Daniel leaves Boing-Boing overnight at the Natural History Museum, to the dismay of a burglar.
    ISBN 1-57498-129-3
    [1. Cats--Fiction. 2. Robots--Fiction. 3. Inventors--Fiction. 4. Museums--Fiction. 5. Robbers and outlaws--Fiction.]   I. Lear, Ruth Denise, ill. II. Title.
    PZ7.H37765 Br 2001
    [Fic]--dc21
                                    2001022443

For more information about The American Ceramic Society or its publications, please call (614) 794-5890 or visit <www.ceramics.org>. Boing-Boing has his own website, too—<www.boing-boing.org>.

For Daniel and Jessica

Contents

BIONIC CAT
DESIGN FEATURES

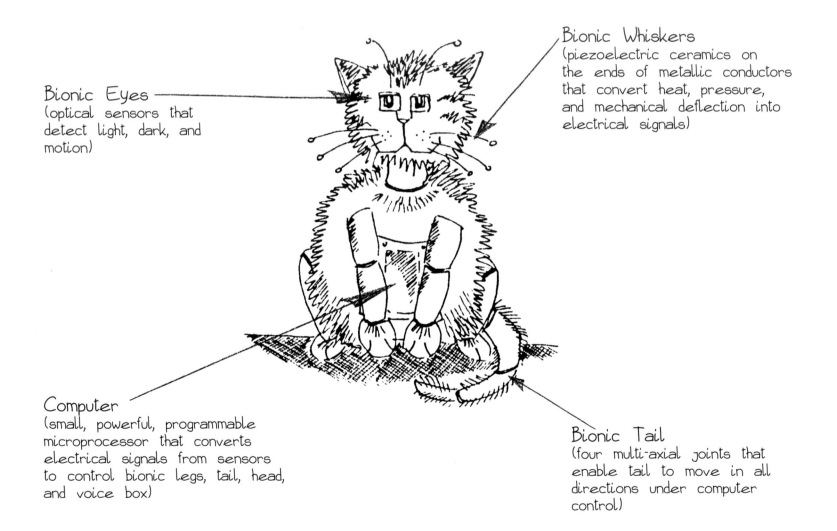

Bionic Whiskers
(piezoelectric ceramics on the ends of metallic conductors that convert heat, pressure, and mechanical deflection into electrical signals)

Bionic Eyes
(optical sensors that detect light, dark, and motion)

Computer
(small, powerful, programmable microprocessor that converts electrical signals from sensors to control bionic legs, tail, head, and voice box)

Bionic Tail
(four multi-axial joints that enable tail to move in all directions under computer control)

10

BIONIC CAT
DESIGN FEATURES

Fiber-Optic Fur
(optical glass fiber, covering all surfaces, that transmits sunlight through the fibers to photoelectric cells that charge the batteries)

Batteries
(6 rechargeable 9-volt batteries that provide power to the computer, the bionic eyes, tail, legs, head, and ceramic heating elements)

Bionic Tail Sensor
(piezoelectric ceramic sensor in tail joint that sends signal to the computer and voice simulator to generate a ROAR with the loudness increasing as pressure on the sensor increases)

Bionic Voice Box
(programmable voice simulator activated by sensors embedded in the fiber-optic fur; controlled by the computer)

Bionic Legs
(4 legs with 3 multi-axial joints per leg connected to small motors controlled by the computer)

Chapter One

Daniel was sitting on his front porch waiting for Professor George to come home from the university. It was getting late and Daniel said to himself, "Poor Professor George, he must be working late again. He does work hard. I'll just have to wait until tomorrow to ask him."

Daniel's mum had come to the door and overheard. "What do you want to ask Professor George, Dan?" she asked.

"Oh, nothing," he replied. Daniel did not want his mother to know what was bothering him.

"Well, it's about time to eat. Come in and wash your hands, Dan."

"OK, Mum," Daniel answered.

Just then, he saw his friend coming round the corner. "Professor George! Professor George!" Daniel shouted as he jumped up to meet him.

"Hello Daniel," said Professor George. "How are you? Why are you so excited?"

"It's Boing-Boing. Something has happened to him. Can you look at him, please?" asked Daniel, holding out his bionic cat to the professor.

"Of course," answered Professor George as he took the bionic cat.

He had made the cat a few months earlier for Daniel, who had been very sad because he could not have a pet cat since he was allergic to them. So, to cheer Daniel up, Professor George had stayed up all night and made the bionic cat from ceramic and electronic parts he had in his workshop. It was a very special cat indeed and Daniel was not allergic to it at all because the cat had fiber-optic fur.

"I don't see anything unusual," Professor George said as he looked at the cat. Everything appeared to be in place. The bionic cat's shiny fur sparkled in the sunlight. The fur was made of very fine glass fibers that carry sunlight to special solar cells inside the cat where the sunlight is converted to energy that charges the bionic cat's batteries.

His special whiskers were in good shape, too. The bionic cat's whiskers, made of very thin wires with special ceramic sensors on the ends, were important because they kept Boing-Boing out of danger. Some of the sensors can feel objects in Boing-Boing's way and let him know to move around them using his battery-driven legs. Other sensors on the whiskers detect heat or cold and warn the cat of danger.

Next, Professor George looked into the bionic cat's eyes that glowed with a soft yellow light. These bionic eyes were connected to a very small computer in the cat's belly. The computer used very little power so the cat can sit still for hours and hours without moving and still be alert and full of energy.

Professor George had made the bionic cat to be just like a real cat, and Daniel loved Boing-Boing very much.

"What's wrong with Boing-Boing, Dan?" asked the professor.

Daniel answered, "Boing-Boing has stopped purring when I pet him.

"See—when I stroke him like this, nothing happens."

Daniel liked to hold Boing-Boing. The bionic cat was slightly warm and his fiber-optic fur was silky soft. When the fur was stroked, the cat would make a gentle "purrr-purrr" sound.

Professor George listened closely to the bionic cat. "You're right, Dan," he said. "There's no sound at all when you pet him. Maybe a wire connecting his voice box to the computer has come loose."

"I don't think that's the problem, Professor George," responded Daniel. "Just listen."

He rubbed his cat's nose and the bionic cat quickly said, "Boing-Boing!" He did it again and the cat repeated, "Boing-Boing!"

Professor George laughed. "I guess you're right, Dan. There's nothing wrong with his

17

voice box or the wiring." He added, "I am still surprised when I hear him say 'Boing-Boing' instead of 'meow-meow' like cats should. I don't know how I made that mistake when I programmed the computer."

"Professor George," said Daniel, "you shouldn't be unhappy because you made a mistake. Boing-Boing is the only cat in the world that says its own name. Boing-Boing is really special. I'm glad he doesn't 'meow-meow' like everyone else's cats."

"Well, I'm happy that you like it so much, Dan. But it is still a little frustrating to me," sighed Professor George.

"Do you think you can fix Boing-Boing so he can purr again?" asked Daniel.

"I'll try," replied Professor George as he took the bionic cat from Daniel.

"Promise you won't stop Boing-Boing from saying his name!" Daniel called out as his friend walked away.

I promise," said Professor George, already wondering what was wrong with the cat.

After dinner Professor George said to his wife, "Honey, I'm going downstairs to my workshop for a little while to see if I can fix Boing-Boing for Dan."

"All right," she answered. "Just make sure you don't lose track of time. Promise you won't stay down there all night like you did when you built Boing-Boing. You have an early class in the morning."

"I promise," he answered as he started down the steps.

19

Chapter Two

Professor George walked down to his basement workshop. It was a very special workshop—a small version of the bioengineering research lab that he directed at the university.

On his workbench were many tools and special ceramic parts. He also had lots of electronic equipment and a powerful computer, nicknamed Supie, which was connected to the big super computer at the university.

Professor George turned on his computer, typed in his passwords and said, partly to himself and partly to the computer, "Well, Supie, let's see what's wrong with Boing-Boing."

He unscrewed the small plate in the bionic cat's belly and opened the compartment containing the cat's little computer. Next, he attached some wires from his computer to the bionic cat.

"OK, Supie," he muttered. "Show me what's wrong with this little guy."

The computer screen lit up with a colored display of the wiring inside Boing-Boing.

Professor George used the mouse connected to the computer to follow the circuit controlling the voice simulator.

"Hey, isn't that funny," he chuckled to himself. "I'm using a mouse to fix a cat! Dan will get a real laugh at that when I tell him tomorrow.

"There it is!" exclaimed Professor George, peering closely at the computer screen. "A piece of dust is causing a short between two wires. That's why you're not purring, little fellow. No problem, I can fix you in no time at all."

After removing the dust with a pair of tweezers, Professor George said to himself, "Aha, I have an idea. I'll add a nice surprise to Boing-Boing for Dan."

So, he began typing some changes into the computer program that controlled Boing-Boing's voice simulator.

Professor George finished and put Boing-Boing on the floor. "There! You're even more special now. Let's see how your new talent works."

He tested the change and laughed at the results.

"Yes, indeed. Boing-Boing, you will really give Dan a big surprise tomorrow. Now, I must look at tomorrow's lecture notes and then to bed."

Chapter Three

The next evening Daniel was waiting eagerly on his front steps. "Professor George! Professor George!" he called when he saw his friend. "Is Boing-Boing OK?"

"He sure is," answered Professor George. "Come, and I'll show you. In fact, he's even better than before."

"Oh, no!" responded Daniel. "You didn't stop him saying 'Boing-Boing' did you?"

"Of course not, Dan," said Professor George. "Remember, I promised you I wouldn't."

"Yes," said Daniel. "I'm sorry."

Professor George took Daniel down to his workshop.

Daniel picked up the bionic cat and switched him on. He stroked the fiber-optic fur and heard a very pleasant "purrr-purrr."

"Great," said Daniel. Then he rubbed the bionic cat's nose and heard **"Boing-Boing, Boing-Boing."**

"Super!" Daniel exclaimed. "You're right, Professor George. He's as good as new."

"Wrong," replied the professor. "He's better than new. Here, I'll show you."

Professor George put the bionic cat on the floor. The cat's tail slowly switched back and forth.

"Watch, Dan," he said. "After a few minutes the tail will stop since the cat is not moving."

"That's neat!" said Daniel.

"The best is yet to come," responded Professor George. "Squeeze Boing-Boing's tail very gently and see what happens."

Daniel ever so gently squeezed his cat's tail and then jumped back with a fright as Boing-Boing let out a great big "**Roar!**"

"WOW!" shouted Daniel. "How did he do that?"

Professor George laughed and said, "I put a new ceramic sensor in Boing-Boing's tail and programmed another set of commands to his voice simulator, Dan.

"Squeeze his tail a little bit harder—not too hard though! You don't want to break his fiber-optic fur."

Daniel very carefully squeezed the tail, this time a little bit harder.

He jumped back again as Boing-Boing let out an even louder **"Roarr!!"**

"WOW!" Daniel shouted again. "This is unbelievable. Boing-Boing sounds just like the lion I saw in the zoo. He is awesome. He is really scary!"

"You need to be careful, Dan, about using this new talent of Boing-Boing's," cautioned Professor George. "You shouldn't frighten people just for fun. But it can be useful if you or your cat is in danger."

"I'll say," responded Daniel. "His roar would surprise anyone, anytime. Thanks a lot Professor George. You do invent some clever things. I'll see you tomorrow."

Chapter Four

The next morning was Saturday.
Daniel woke up, yawned, and
looked at Boing-Boing sitting
on the windowsill, soaking up
the sunshine.

He picked up his bionic cat
and gently stroked his fur.
Boing-Boing said, "Purrr-purrr."

"Great!" thought Daniel.
"You're still OK."

He then *very, very* gently squeezed his
bionic cat's tail. "**Roar!**" responded the cat, sounding just like a fierce lion.

Daniel was glad he had only squeezed the tail a little bit. He did not want his mother to be alarmed.

"Wow! If I gave your tail a really hard squeeze, your roar could be heard all the way to Professor George's house," thought Daniel. "I really need to remember to be careful."

After breakfast Daniel's mother asked, "Dan, do you still want to go to the museum today?"

"Yes!" he replied. "I've been waiting all week."

"Are you certain that you can get there and back by yourself?" asked his mother.

"Of course I can," said Daniel. "You've taken me there many times. I could do it in my sleep."

"All right, you can go on your own this time," his mother said. "But be sure to call if you get lost, and be home by three o'clock. No later or I'll worry."

"OK, Mummy, I promise," replied Daniel as he ran from the room.

When Daniel got to his room he took his bionic cat from the windowsill and asked, "Boing-Boing, would you like to go to the museum with me?

"Bye, Mummy," he called out as he left the house with his bionic cat. "I'll be home by three o'clock."

A few blocks away, Daniel
caught the bus that took him to
the Natural History Museum. As he rode along, he watched out the window and
petted Boing-Boing. His bionic cat felt nice and warm and purred very happily.

At the museum, Daniel bounded up three flights of steps. The Natural History Museum was a very large building that used to frighten Daniel when he was little. The twin towers seemed to reach to the sky and the stone animal carvings all around the building scared him. Now, though, the museum was one of his favorite places. Daniel went through the large wooden doors and entered the huge central hall.

He turned left and looked up. High, high above him towered the skeleton of a dinosaur. It was huge, as tall as a four-story building. Daniel stopped to read the sign. "I remember this, it is a Diplodocus," he told Boing-Boing. "I saw these on TV, but this real skeleton is much more impressive.

"This dinosaur was just about the largest animal to have walked on earth, and it ate hundreds of pounds of plants every day."

Nearby was Tyrannosaurus Rex, the fiercest dinosaur of them all. It had the biggest teeth and the strongest jaws, and was believed to be a mean, mad eating-machine that preyed on the dinosaurs that ate plants.

"T-Rex, you sure are huge," said Daniel, as he looked up at the 35-foot high, reconstructed dinosaur. "Your teeth are as big as my cat. I'm glad you're not alive now. You could eat me up in one bite."

Daniel walked all around T-Rex, taking one last look

33

at him. He was imagining what life was like millions of years ago.

As he turned to go on, Daniel clutched his bag tightly. Then he jumped with fright. He thought he had seen T-Rex look down at him and roar.

Daniel clutched his bag even tighter. This time, he was certain he heard a frightening roar coming from the huge dinosaur.

Daniel's eyes got very big. He turned pale. His teeth started to chatter. He tried to run but couldn't. His legs would not move a step. His feet felt like they were glued to the ground. He began to tremble and clutched his bag even tighter. Again he heard an even louder **"Roarrr!"**

He was sure that T-Rex was going to pick him up and eat him. He yelled, "Help! Help! Someone, help!"

A museum guard came running. "What's the matter young man?" he asked. "What's wrong?"

"I'm s-s-so glad to see you. I thought for s-s-sure I s-s-saw that huge dinosaur m-m-move and r-r-roar at me," stammered Daniel.

"Well, I agree he does look real," answered the guard. "But I assure you that he has not moved or roared for as long as I can remember."

"But I heard him roar," pleaded Daniel. "I really did."

"It must have been your imagination. Tyrannosaurus Rex was alive about 65 million years ago. He has not roared for a long, long time, and he's just a skeleton now, like all the others you see here.

"OK? Have you seen the whales yet? They won't frighten you. Why don't you run along now?"

"Thanks a lot," replied Daniel. "I guess it must have been my imagination. But, it sure sounded like a real roar. I'll go see the whales next. Thanks, again. Bye."

BLUE WHALE

Chapter Five

Daniel went quickly into the hall nearby, called Whale Hall.

"WOW!" he exclaimed. "I'd forgotten just how big whales are."

He was looking at both the skeleton and the recreation of a blue whale that filled the center of the hall.

The sign said:

> Whales are mammals. They are not fishes even though they look similar to fishes. The blue whale is the largest mammal to have ever lived on earth. It can be more than 100 feet long.

Daniel, remembering another museum he had visited, said "Mister whale, guess what? You're even bigger than a train engine. I wonder how many carloads of fish you can pull?

The next sign read:

> Whales, ultimately, get their energy from sunlight. The sunlight is converted to small plants, called plankton. The plankton is eaten by very small shrimp-like animals, called krill, and the whales eat the krill. They eat tons of krill, roaming the seas of the world in search of food.

"WOW!" he thought. "Boing-Boing and a blue whale have something in common—their energy comes from the sun! Boing-Boing gets his energy from the sunlight that travels through his fiber-optic fur, converts to electricity, and charges his batteries. And the blue whale gets energy from the sun, but by eating the krill." Daniel remarked, "Nature is fantastic."

The next sign Daniel and Boing-Boing saw told them:

Whales breathe air to live. When a whale comes to the surface to spout, it is exhaling carbon dioxide. The whale then breathes in air containing oxygen before it dives.

"That is really cool," said Daniel. "Whales breathe in air to live just like I do! That is a big difference between Boing-Boing and this big blue whale," concluded Daniel. "Boing-Boing doesn't breathe in oxygen or breathe out carbon dioxide. He lives without breathing at all. That's another reason he's a bionic cat instead of a real cat."

After a while Daniel grew tired of looking at the whales and went into the next room.

"Oh boy!" he said, "these are my favorites!"

He looked around and tried to decide which was best. He was surrounded with sharks, dozens of species of sharks.

There were little sharks, medium-sized sharks, and even the giant whale shark that can grow to 40 feet long.

"It's a good thing they are all stuffed," said Daniel. "I wouldn't like to have another scare like I did with T-Rex. I wonder why I heard that roar?"

Then Daniel remembered. "Of course! I bet it was Boing-Boing."

So he clutched his bag a little harder. "**Roar!**" went the bag.

Daniel opened it and looked in. "Boing-Boing are you unhappy in there? How silly of me to have forgotten about your new talent. No wonder that museum guard thought I was a little crazy.

"How would you like to see some really neat fishes, Boing-Boing?" asked Daniel. "I bet a bionic cat likes fishes, even if you don't eat them like real cats do."

So Daniel showed Boing-Boing the various species of sharks. "See, there's a nurse shark, and a mako shark, and a tiger shark, and a hammerhead shark. WOW. Boing-Boing, look at the jaws of this great white shark. Its teeth are almost as big as those of T-Rex. I guess it is the T-Rex of the seas. I wonder if Professor George could make a bionic shark? That would be really exciting," said Daniel.

Chapter Six

Then Daniel asked, "How would you like to see some of your relatives, Boing-Boing?"

He gave the bag a small squeeze and Boing-Boing responded with a tiny **"roar."**

"OK, let's go," he said as they went looking for the animals in the cat family.

"Here are your aunts, uncles, and cousins, Boing-Boing," said Daniel. "WOW! They are really big."

He looked around the balcony of the central hall and saw a jaguar, a leopard, a lion, a tiger, and a cheetah. He also saw something very unusual.

"Look, Boing-Boing. Here's one of your ancestors from thousands of years ago—a saber-toothed tiger. It is extinct; no more live anywhere on earth. WOW!"

"Those incisor teeth are awesome! They are even bigger than those of the great white shark and T-Rex!"

Next, Daniel stopped in front of the lion. "The lion is called the king of the jungle, Boing-Boing. Can you imagine what a bionic lion would be like? I could ride it to and from school. The other kids would be even more surprised than when I took you to school for 'Show and Tell.' I'll ask Professor George if he can build a bionic lion."

Just then Daniel had another idea. "Boing-Boing, would you like to sit down next to your big aunts and uncles? I'd like to see how you look compared to these big cats."

So, Daniel took Boing-Boing out of his bag and set him down near the stuffed lion.

He stepped back to look at his cat and compare it with the huge wild cats.

Daniel forgot that his bionic cat was turned on with nearly a full battery charge.

Boing-Boing's tail switched a few times, then he became still, his eyes glowing slightly.

Just then a museum guard came around the corner. It was the same guard who had helped Daniel earlier. "Well young man, I see that you are not frightened of the jungle cats. They are more fierce today than dinosaurs, you know."

"I know, sir. It was silly of me to be scared by T-Rex. It won't happen again," Daniel responded.

"You need to run on home now," instructed the guard. "It's closing time."

"Oh no!" cried Daniel. "I'll be in real trouble. I promised my mum I'd be home by three o'clock. She'll be really worried."

"It's much later than that," said the guard. "I'll tell you what will help. There's a phone nearby. You can give her a call and tell her not to worry."

"Thank you. Thank you very much," responded Daniel. "She will be ever so grateful."

Daniel went off quickly with the guard to make the call. He was so worried that he forgot all about Boing-Boing sitting quietly next to the lion.

It was only after Daniel was on the bus that he felt his bag and realized it was empty.

He turned cold all over. He knew right away that he had left Boing-Boing in the museum. A big tear rolled down his cheek. "What am I going to do?" he cried.

Chapter Seven

When Daniel arrived home he knew he was in big trouble. He had lots of explaining and apologizing to do. "I'm sorry Mummy," he said, sobbing. "I forgot all about the time. I really didn't mean to be bad. I was just so interested in everything that I forgot to look at the clock. Then, to make it even worse, I forgot Boing-Boing. Are you going to punish me?"

His mother replied, "Leaving your bionic cat in the museum overnight is creating your own punishment, Daniel. That's what often happens to people, even grown-ups. We do something we shouldn't and then suffer the consequences. This should be a real lesson to you about what happens when you are irresponsible."

"What will happen to Boing-Boing, Mummy? Maybe the museum will throw him away by mistake!" pleaded Daniel.

"I doubt that, Daniel, but let's try to call anyway," suggested his mother.

After the phone rang many times, she finally said, "No luck. We'll just have to wait until the museum opens tomorrow and we'll go get him then."

Daniel went to bed that night very sad and very worried. He hoped that Boing-Boing would be OK all alone in the museum.

But Boing-Boing was not all alone.

Late that night something very exciting happened, and Boing-Boing was right in the middle of it. In fact, what happened that night made Boing-Boing the most famous cat in the country.

It was about two o'clock in the morning. The museum was very quiet. All the cleaning crew had come and gone. Only one guard remained, and he was slowly making his rounds inspecting the museum's many rooms.

Slowly, ever so slowly, a door opened from a passageway between the Natural History Museum and the Geological Museum.

A man slipped through that door without making a sound.

He was dressed all in black—even his sneakers. He had a black mask covering everything but his eyes. He had a black stocking cap pulled down over his ears and he was carrying a large black bag. The bag was full and very heavy.

The man had been
hiding in an old,
forgotten storeroom
in the basement of
the Geological
Museum. When
everyone had gone,
he disabled all the
alarms. Then, one
by one, he opened
the jewel cases
displayed in the
museum and removed
all of the very
best gems.

He took rubies, sapphires, and emeralds. Then he took the biggest and best diamonds. The jewels, all very old and rare, were some of the best in the world. It would be a terrible loss for the museum to have these precious gems stolen.

But the burglar's plans were not perfect and he was in trouble. A delivery truck blocked his escape. He tried the door. It opened two inches, just enough to get his arm through. He tried again and almost got his head stuck!

Then the man remembered a small fire escape from the balcony, with a narrow ladder leading down to the ground. All he had to do was get there without the guard discovering him.

He silently sneaked along the hallway to the stairs leading up to the balcony. He stopped and listened very carefully. All was silent. "So far, so good," he whispered to himself. "Nothing here . . . just a bunch of dead animals. They can't hurt me. It looks like I'm safe."

He looked around and saw the gigantic dinosaurs nearby. "I'm sure glad they're dead," he whispered nervously.

Slowly, the thief worked his way up to the balcony. Once there, he stopped and looked around. The moon was shining through a skylight so he could see a little better here. But, there were also lots of very dark shadows.

"Wow," he muttered to himself as he saw the family of jungle cats. "I'm glad those creatures are dead, too. They're worse than any dinosaur."

The man looked at the door with its Fire Escape sign glowing red above it.

He started toward the door, stepping very carefully through the exhibit of large, wild cats.

He never noticed the two eyes following him. They were glowing slightly yellow and saw the man very clearly, even in the dark.

The thief never saw the tail start to switch back and forth as he stepped around the huge lion.

He never saw his foot land, and he never saw it step right on top of the tail.

But, the burglar certainly did hear the result—

"ROARRR!"

Boing-Boing let out a roar that echoed back and forth across the huge hall.

The burglar's head was only inches from the lion's teeth, and that's all he saw. Lots and lots of teeth. Big, sharp pointed teeth. And all of them meant just for him.

Well, what do you think the thief did? You're right. He did what anyone else would do. He screamed— loud and long.

He yelled "HELLLP!" so loudly that he drowned out Boing-Boing's roar. Then he turned and ran.

"LET ME OUT! Let me out! Let me out!" he yelled, as he scrambled down the steps with jewels flying out of his bag all the way. His foot slipped on a couple of big red rubies and he bounced down the rest of the steps.

BOOM! BOOM! BOOM! He landed at the bottom, right at the feet of the museum guard.

The guard was a fan of old movies and liked a good joke. He shone his flashlight on the thief and the light sparkled back at him from the bright red gems.

"Well, what do we have here? It looks like Dorothy and her ruby slippers.

"Well buddy, whoever you are, you sure missed the Yellow Brick Road and this sure ain't Kansas! But, you are goin' to need a wizard to get out of this fix!"

The guard quickly put handcuffs on the man, who kept pleading, "Don't let him eat me! Don't let him eat me!"

Chapter Eight

Later that morning Daniel and his mother arrived at the museum as it opened. Daniel asked the guard who was still there, "Excuse me sir, I left my bionic cat here yesterday. May I go look for him?"

"So young man, you're the one who left that mechanical cat here. I think you had better come with me."

Daniel and his mum followed the guard to the museum director's office. The director was there along with several reporters, three policemen, and a detective from Scotland Yard. They all looked very serious. Daniel felt very small indeed. He was very worried and became even more scared when the director stood up. Daniel had not expected this much trouble. "Oh-oh," he thought. "This is worse than T-Rex was yesterday."

"Young man, is this yours?" asked the director, pointing to Boing-Boing sitting on his desk.

Daniel answered, "Yes sir, it's mine. Professor George made it for me."

"Do you know what your cat did last night?" the director asked.

"No," replied Daniel in a very small voice. "I hope it wasn't something bad."

"On the contrary, young man," said the director, "Your cat is the biggest hero this museum has ever had. He helped catch a jewel thief who almost escaped with our very best gems."

"How did that happen?" asked Daniel.

The guard answered, "The thief apparently stepped on your cat as he was sneaking through the wild cat exhibit. We're not sure why, but he became very scared and then screamed for help. He ran away, slipped on the stairs, and fell right at my feet—the easiest arrest I've ever made. He pleaded with me to get him away from there. He was really scared."

Daniel thought for a minute and remembered where he had left Boing-Boing. He said, "I bet I know what happened—the thief thought that the huge lion was going to eat him."

"Why would he think that?" the detective from Scotland Yard asked in disbelief.

60

"Here, I'll show you," replied Daniel as he reached over and picked up Boing-Boing. He took hold of his bionic cat's tail and gave it a really hard squeeze.

Boing-Boing responded instantly: "ROARRR!"

Everyone in the room jumped back.

"That is a very special cat you have, young man," said the director regaining his composure. "You must take better care of it.

"Now, as a token of our appreciation, we have something special for both of you."

With that, he opened a box and removed two medals on ribbons. The bigger one he put around Daniel's neck and the smaller one he put around Boing-Boing's neck.

"You are both now honorary members of the museum for life," said the director as he shook Daniel's hand.

"Thank you very much," responded Daniel with a big smile.

The director then reached down to shake the cat's paw and accidentally rubbed the cat's nose.

The bionic cat looked up at him and said, **"Boing-Boing."**

The director replied,
"Little fellow, that's the
nicest 'thank you' I've
ever had.

"Now, young man, is
there anything else you
would like to say?"
asked the director.

"Yes," replied Daniel, "I
think I know why Boing-Boing
was able to catch the jewel thief."

"Why?" asked one of the reporters.

"Because he was a *cat* burglar!" answered Daniel, laughing.

The End

Maybe yes and maybe no . . .

. . . only time will tell!

About the Author

Larry L. Hench, Ph.D., served as professor of ceramic engineering for 32 years at The University of Florida, and is currently professor of ceramic materials at Imperial College of Science, Technology, and Medicine at the University of London and director of the Imperial College Centre for Tissue Regeneration and Repair.

Recently inducted into the U.S. National Academy of Engineering, Hench will advise the U.S. government on a wide range of scientific, social, and medical issues.

A world-renowned scientist, graduate of The Ohio State University, and Fellow of The American Ceramic Society—Hench's numerous achievements, honors, scholarly writings, and patents, over his 40-year career, span several fields including: ceramics, glass and glass-ceramic materials, radiation damage, nuclear waste solidification, advanced optical materials, origins of life, ethics, technology transfer, and bioceramics applications and mechanisms.

He is credited with the discovery of Bioglass®, the first man-made material to bond to living bone—helping millions of people; and he continues to discover new applications in bioceramics for this amazing material. Hench is currently working with students to find the genes that are activated by bioactive glasses and ceramics. Once these genes are found, he hopes to develop preventive treatments to stop deterioration of bones in people as they grow older.

His children's books extend his love of teaching and science and engineering to a new generation. Everything built into the stories is scientifically valid and could be done. The inspiration for these books comes from his nine grandchildren.

Hench, an Ohio native, now divides his time between London and the United States. He and his wife, June Wilson, share four children and nine grandchildren.

About the illustrator

Ruth Denise Lear was born in Wilmslow, Cheshire, England, in 1965, and lives now with her husband and three children in a rural village on the outskirts of Macclesfield, Cheshire.

Her love of drawing began in childhood and has never left her. She studied at Macclesfield College and has produced and sold paintings, cards, and etchings. Her favorite media are watercolor and ink, which have been used for the Boing-Boing series.

"This (my) second book has been quite exciting for me, as Daniel and Boing-Boing meet such a wide range of creatures in the story—many of which I have never had the pleasure of drawing before!"

We think you'll enjoy them!

About The American Ceramic Society

The American Ceramic Society (ACerS) serves its members and the worldwide ceramic community by promoting the development and use of ceramics through forums for knowledge exchange.

As the world's leading organization dedicated to the advancement of ceramics, ACerS serves more than 10,000 members and subscribers in 80 countries. ACerS' members include ceramic engineers, scientists, researchers, educators, students, sales and production personnel, manufacturers, artists, and others in the ceramics and related materials industry. Founded in 1898, ACerS provides the latest technical, scientific, and educational information to its members and other constituencies. Visit our website <www.ceramics.org> for more information.